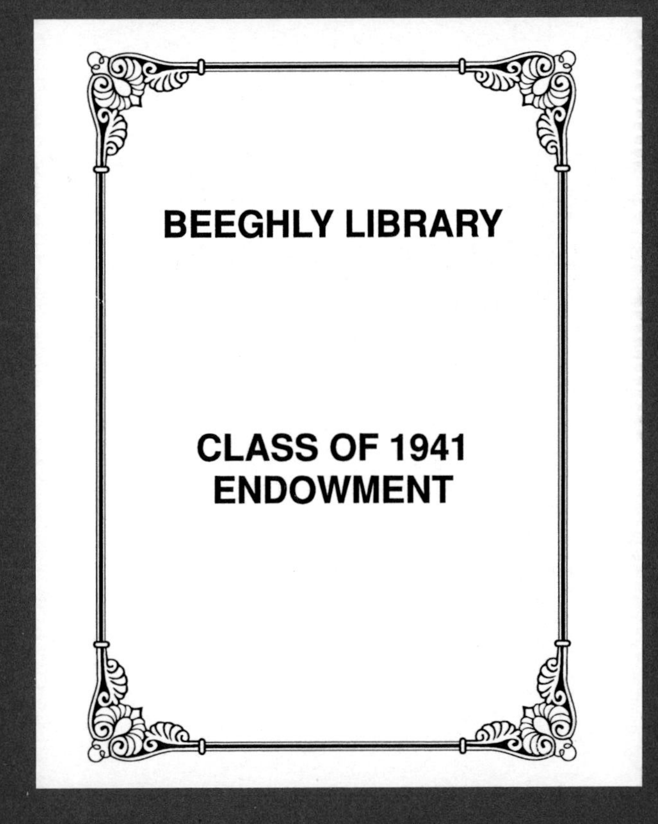
BEEGHLY LIBRARY
CLASS OF 1941
ENDOWMENT

DODSWORTH IN LONDON

Written and illustrated by

TIM EGAN

HOUGHTON MIFFLIN BOOKS FOR CHILDREN
HOUGHTON MIFFLIN HARCOURT
BOSTON NEW YORK 2009

For Bernie and Babe

Houghton Mifflin Books for Children is an imprint of Houghton Mifflin Harcourt Publishing Company.

www.hmhbooks.com

The text of this book is set in Cochin.
The illustrations are ink and watercolor on paper.

Library of Congress Catalog Control Number 2008040464

ISBN: 978-0-547-13816-9

Printed in Singapore
TWP 10 9 8 7 6 5 4 3 2 1

CONTENTS

CHAPTER ONE

A FOGGY MORNING

Dodsworth and the duck had traveled all the way from Paris, France.
As the balloon floated over England, Dodsworth saw Buckingham Palace through the fog.
"That's where the queen lives," he said.
The duck was impressed.

"Let's stay there," said the duck.

"We can't stay there," said Dodsworth.

"Why not?" asked the duck.

"Because it's Buckingham Palace,"
said Dodsworth. "It's not a motel."

The balloon landed in Trafalgar Square.

"Now, stay close to me," said Dodsworth.

"I don't want to lose you in the fog."

"Who said that?" said the duck.

"Very funny," said Dodsworth.

They walked down Charing Cross Road.

"This is the best," said Dodsworth.

"Where should we go first?"

"Food sounds good," said the duck.

"I agree," said Dodsworth.

They strolled near Picadilly Circus.

They saw a classic old pub.

"Perfect," said Dodsworth.

They walked into the pub.

The pub was very loud.

Some folks were eating.

Some folks were throwing darts.

Some folks were playing cards.

The duck liked the darts.

The duck looked at a dart.

Dodsworth looked at the duck.

"Don't even think about it," he said.

The duck smiled.

The duck grabbed the dart.

Dodsworth jumped at the duck.

He wasn't fast enough.

The duck threw the dart.

The dart hit a book.

The book hit a waiter.

The waiter dropped a pie

onto a lady's head.

It was not good.

The pub became very quiet.
The crowd stared at Dodsworth
and the duck.
It was time to leave.

CHAPTER TWO

THE BUS STATION

"I can't believe you!" yelled Dodsworth. "We just got here and you're already causing trouble!"

"I'm sorry," said the duck.

Dodsworth didn't believe him.

A large red double-decker bus drove by.
“That’s the greatest bus I’ve ever seen,”
said the duck.
Dodsworth smiled.
“And the perfect way to see London,”
he said. “I can keep an eye on you.”

They walked to the bus station.
The duck saw another duck in the crowd.
The other duck looked exactly like him, except for his fancy hat.

Many folks got off the bus.

Many folks got on the bus.

The area became very crowded.

"Let's wait for the next bus," said

Dodsworth. The duck didn't hear him.

The duck got on the bus.

Dodsworth didn't see him.

The duck saw Dodsworth on the sidewalk.

"Uh-oh," he said.

The bus started pulling away.

"I'll meet you at Buckingham Palace!"
shouted the duck.
Dodsworth didn't hear him.
The bus disappeared into the fog.

Dodsworth turned and saw the other duck, the one with the fancy hat. He looked exactly like his duck. Dodsworth thought it *was* his duck.

“Hey, where did you get that hat?” asked Dodsworth.

“It was a gift from the queen,” said the wrong duck.

He spoke with a British accent.

Dodsworth laughed.

“Nice accent,” he said. “Very convincing.”

He *still* thought it was his duck.

CHAPTER THREE

TOURING LONDON

Another bus pulled up.

The wrong duck walked up to the top of the bus.

Dodsworth followed him.

"This is the greatest," said Dodsworth.

The duck smiled politely.

"You're awfully quiet," said Dodsworth.

"Is everything okay?"

"Splendid," said the duck. "I don't believe we've met. I am the Royal Duck," he said. "The queen's duck."

Dodsworth laughed.

"You're ridiculous," he said.

He *still* thought it was his duck.

The bus drove around London.

"Hey, look," said Dodsworth. "It's London Bridge."

"Actually, that's Tower Bridge," said the duck. "London Bridge is just up the river a bit."

Dodsworth looked at him.

"How do you know that?" asked Dodsworth.

"It's common knowledge," said the duck.

Dodsworth just shook his head.

A moment later, Dodsworth said, "Look, there's Big Ben. Now, *that's* a clock."

"Indeed," said the duck, "although its proper name is the Clock Tower. Big Ben is the name of the giant bell inside."

“What?!” said Dodsworth.

“How in the world do you know that?”

“I studied at Oxford,” said the duck.

Dodsworth looked confused.

"Okay, what's going on here?" asked Dodsworth. "You never went to Oxford. How is your accent so perfect? Why aren't you being silly, like always?"

“I’m afraid I don’t understand,” said the duck. “I am the Royal Duck. Her Majesty’s Duck. I honestly have no idea who you are.”

And as the bus drove along the River Thames, Dodsworth finally realized that this was *not* his duck.

Dodsworth went into a panic.
“Where’s my duck?!” he shouted.
“I have a friend who looks exactly like you, except for the hat, and I’ve lost him! This can’t be happening!”

"Now, now," said the Royal Duck.
"Stay calm. We'll find your friend.
I'll have the bus turn around."

The bus raced back to the station.

The duck was not there.

"What am I going to do?" said Dodsworth.

He was very upset.

"I'll ring Scotland Yard," said the duck.

A moment later, a police car pulled up.

"Okay," asked a detective, "what does the duck look like?"

"Like him!" shouted Dodsworth.

"He looks exactly like him!"

Dodsworth was beside himself.

"I don't even know where to start looking," he said.

"We'll find him," said the Royal Duck.

"Trust me."

They all hopped in the car and started searching all over London.

Down by the Parliament.

Over in Kensington Gardens.

Up by the Royal Academy.

There was no sign of him anywhere.

They looked for eight hours straight.

The sun was setting.

The duck was nowhere to be found.

Dodsworth fought back tears.

“I can’t take this,” he said.

“What if he’s hurt? What if he’s scared?

“What if I never find him?”

He was a nervous wreck.

CHAPTER FOUR

BUCKINGHAM PALACE

All this time, Dodsworth's duck was just fine.

He was slowly making his way to Buckingham Palace.

He saw a Shakespeare play in the park.

He had crumpets and tea for lunch.

He splashed in the fountain near Pershing Square.

He was asked to leave Pershing Square.

He finally made it to Buckingham Palace. The guards at the palace were very serious. The duck did a little dance to make them laugh. The guards opened the gates.

Meanwhile, still searching, Dodsworth
was sick with worry.
"I can't believe this," he whispered.
"I've lost my friend . . ."
He dropped to the ground in grief.

“There, there,” said the Royal Duck.

He thought for a moment.

“Perhaps the queen can help,” he said.

“Driver, take us to the palace at once!”

They raced to Buckingham Palace.

The Royal Duck ran up to the gates.

"Hold on there," said the guard.

"But I am the Royal Duck," said the duck.

"Nice try," said the guard.

“The Royal Duck has been here for hours,” said the guard. “But you do look exactly like him.”

“Wait a minute,” said Dodsworth.

“My duck!” he shouted.

He burst through the gates.

The Royal Duck followed him.

Dodsworth ran into the Grand Ballroom.
His duck was dancing on the piano.
The queen was clapping along.
"You're right," said the Royal Duck.
"He does look *exactly* like me."

Dodsworth ran and hugged the duck.

The duck didn't really like to be hugged.

"Is this your duck?" asked the queen.

"He's positively delightful!"

Everything was explained to everyone.
It took about twenty minutes.
"What a wonderful story," said the queen. "You must stay here for the week.
I insist!"
Dodsworth and the duck were speechless.

The Royal Duck showed them to their room.
It was the most magnificent room they had ever seen.
"Enjoy your stay," he said.
"We can't thank you enough," said Dodsworth.

The thick fog rolled in again.
"I'm just happy you're okay," said Dodsworth.
"Who said that?" said the duck.
Dodsworth laughed and hugged the duck again.
And this time, as the night fell on London, the duck actually hugged him back.